Cold Whispers II

The GHOSTLY SECRET of LAKESIDE SCHOOL

by Dee Phillips

illustrated by Amit Tayal

BEARPORT PUBLISHING

New York, New York

Credits

Cover, © liam1949/Shutterstock, © gallofoto/Shutterstock, © Roman Tsubin/ Shutterstock, © 1000 Words/Shutterstock, and © Cory A. Ulrich/Shutterstock.

Publisher: Kenn Goin
Senior Editor: Joyce Tavolacci
Creative Director: Spencer Brinker

Library of Congress Cataloging-in-Publication Data in process at time of publication (2017)
Library of Congress Control Number: 2016019102
ISBN-13: 978-1-944102-33-3

For more information, write to Bearport Publishing Company, Inc., 45 West 21st Street, Suite 3B, New York, New York 10010. Printed in the United States of America.

10 9 8 7 6 5 4 3 2 1

Contents

CHAPTER 1

The Voice

It was Maddie's second week at her new school, and she was hanging out with her new friends—Christa and Evie. As the three girls ate lunch in the cafeteria, Christa and Evie were telling Maddie all about Lakeside Middle School.

"Mr. Martin is nice," said Christa, scooping mac and cheese into her mouth. "But he gives out more homework than any other teacher."

"Mrs. Joseph is . . . ," Evie chimed in. She looked over her shoulder to make sure she wasn't being overheard. "She's so strict. Can you believe she's been teaching here for 30 years?"

Maddie smiled at her two new friends. Her family had moved to the small town of Lakeside just weeks before, and she'd been really nervous about going to a new school. But she was beginning to feel more comfortable.

Maddie looked around at the school's weathered brick walls. "So how old is this place?" she asked her friends.

"Oh. It's ancient," said Evie, making a face. "It's at least one hundred years old."

Maddie's last school was very **modern**. The corridors were painted in bright colors, and the classrooms had enormous windows that let in lots of light. Lakeside couldn't be more different. The building had four floors and windows that made the classrooms feel dark and **claustrophobic**. The long corridors and steep stairways were narrow and gloomy. From the outside, the school reminded Maddie of a haunted house.

5

Despite the school's spooky appearance, Lakeside had a brand-new indoor swimming pool. It also had a music room with a beautiful grand piano. Swimming and playing the piano were Maddie's two favorite things in the world.

Maddie was just about to ask her friends a question about Lakeside's swimming team when Christa motioned for Maddie to lean closer.

"Have you heard about the weird stuff that goes on here?" asked Christa in a hushed voice.

Evie stopped eating and carefully watched to see Maddie's reaction.

"People say they hear footsteps behind them in the hallways," whispered Christa. "But when they turn around, no one's there."

"And," said Evie, "sometimes, people hear other strange things, like . . ."

"What kinds of strange things?" Maddie interrupted.

But before Evie could answer, a loud bell rang. It was time for the girls to hurry back to class.

All afternoon, Maddie wondered what Evie was going to say.

At the end of the school day, Christa and Evie asked Maddie if she wanted to hang out.

"I wish I could. But I booked some practice time in the music room," Maddie explained. She'd never had the chance to play a grand piano—and couldn't wait to try.

Maddie said goodbye to her friends and headed up the main staircase to the fourth floor. At the top of the building was a long, shadowy hallway that led to the music room.

Maddie walked along the corridor. She opened the door to the music room and stepped inside. The big black piano stood in the center of the large, dimly lit room like a crouched animal.

As Maddie walked around the piano, she ran her hand through a layer of dust that covered the shiny black wood. She noticed a huge silvery cobweb under the piano's lid. It was clear that no one had played the piano in a very long time. Maddie slid onto the wooden piano stool and gently touched the black and white keys.

Taking a deep breath, Maddie began to play her favorite piece of music. She knew every note by heart and soon the wonderful sound of the old piano was filling the room.

"*Maddie*," a voice whispered out of nowhere.

Maddie stopped playing. *What was that? Did someone just say my name?* She listened carefully, but the room was silent. She began to play again. Suddenly, the room felt icy cold.

"*You play very well*," whispered a quiet voice behind her.

Maddie jumped up and spun around so fast she knocked the piano stool over. "Who's there?" she demanded.

Maddie's eyes darted from one shadowy corner of the room to the next. There was no one else in the music room. So where was the voice coming from?

"*Maddie, can we be friends?*" said the whisperer.

"Who said that?!" pleaded Maddie. Her voice echoed around the cold, still room. She began to back away from the piano toward the door. This had to be some kind of joke.

"*Don't go, Maddie,*" said the voice, this time a little louder. "*I need your help.*"

Maddie couldn't bear to stay in the music room a moment longer. She grabbed her bag and ran out of the door and down the hallway.

At the top of the stairway, Maddie stopped to catch her breath. Then she heard something. It was coming from the music room. The hairs on the back of her neck prickled.

Someone was playing the old piano. And it was the same song Maddie had just been playing!

Terrified, Maddie raced down the stairs and out into the schoolyard.

Some older kids were chatting in the yard. Maddie realized how strange she must look as she gasped for air and fought back tears. She took a deep breath to calm herself, and then walked out onto the street.

For just a moment, she turned to look back at the old school building. This morning, she'd been amused by the fact that it looked like a house from a horror movie. Now, with the whispering voice and haunting piano music still ringing in her ears, her amusement turned to **dread**.

CHAPTER 2

The Lost Schoolgirl

Maddie's new home was just a short walk from Lakeside Middle School. Still shaking from her strange encounter in the music room, she hurried along the pathway that snaked around the huge lake, which gave Lakeside its name.

When she opened the front door of her house, Max was waiting in the hallway. He was big with rough black-and-brown fur and enormous ears.

Maddie ruffled his big, fuzzy head. "Did you go to work today, Max?" she asked him, heading for the kitchen. Max nudged Maddie with his huge, wet nose.

"No, he didn't," said Maddie's mom, smiling. She was unpacking bowls and pans from a large box.

Maddie's mom worked as a member of a **search-and-rescue** team—and so did Max. Using his powerful sense of smell, Max helped Maddie's mom find people who were lost or missing. There was one part of their work that Maddie didn't like to think about, though. Sometimes, they had to search for dead bodies!

"How was your day, kiddo? How was piano practice?" asked Maddie's dad, who was sitting at the dining room table tapping away at his computer.

Maddie hesitated for a long time. She wasn't sure what to say.

When Maddie didn't answer, Mom stopped unpacking. "Was school okay, Maddie?" she asked, sounding concerned.

Maddie washed her hands and began hunting for a snack in the refrigerator.

"It was, um, great," she said. "I talked a lot with my new friends, Christa and Evie." Maddie decided she wasn't quite ready to share her strange experience in the music room.

After supper, Maddie wrapped herself in a blanket and curled up on the sofa. She switched on her tablet and decided to do some research on her new school. She was just beginning to feel sleepy, when she came across an old newspaper story.

All Hope Lost For Lakeside Schoolgirl

The story was about a 14-year-old girl named Mary Carter, who was president of her class and a talented piano player. One afternoon in spring 1966, Mary left school at the end of the day—and was never seen again.

Maddie felt a chill run down her spine. She asked her parents if they knew the story about Mary. Mom said she had heard about the disappearance but didn't know many details. Maddie spent the next hour trying to learn more about the lost girl. After little success, Maddie shut down her tablet and went to bed. As she lay in the darkness, Maddie wondered what had happened to poor Mary Carter.

CHAPTER 3

The Mysterious Writing

It was Friday afternoon, and Maddie was late for Mr. Martin's history class. As she **briskly** walked down the long empty hallway, she heard footsteps behind her. The footsteps quickened from a walk to a run. Was someone else late to class?

Maddie quickly turned around to see who was behind her. No one was there. She was alone in the long corridor.

All week Maddie had been trying hard to forget the strange experience she'd had in the music room. Now, the confusion and fear she'd felt came flooding back.

"Hello?" she said quietly. "Is . . . is . . . someone there?"

"Will you be joining us, Maddie?"

Maddie nearly jumped out of her skin.

It was Mr. Martin calling from a doorway at the other end of the corridor. Maddie ran to the classroom while Mr. Martin

held the door open for her. Then she settled into an empty seat at the back of the room.

Maddie took a pen and a new notebook from her bag and tried hard to concentrate on Mr. Martin's voice. No matter how much she tried to focus on the lesson, however, her thoughts kept wandering. Had she imagined the footsteps in the corridor? Where had the voice in the music room come from?

"Maddie," said Mr. Martin, hovering over her desk. "Do you have the homework assignment written down?"

Maddie had been so lost in her thoughts, she didn't realize that the class had ended and her classmates were already shuffling out of the room.

"Um . . . I'm not quite finished. I'm sorry." Maddie scrambled for her pen, feeling her face **flush**.

She opened her notebook and flipped past her notes to a new page. Scrawled across the page in blood-red ink were the words, *I need your help Maddie. Will you be my friend?*

Maddie **frantically** turned the pages to find an empty place to write, but all she could see were the same words written on every page of her notebook.

She felt her eyes filling with tears as Mr. Martin looked down at the ink-covered pages.

"It wasn't me," gasped Maddie. "I didn't write this." As she said the words, Maddie realized how **implausible** it sounded.

"Maddie," said Mr. Martin finally. "We have a lot of material to get through this term. You cannot afford to waste time, okay?"

"We'll discuss this again on Monday," he said. He walked to his desk, picked up his bag, and left the classroom.

Maddie threw her notebook into her backpack and hurried out of the room. Just as she left the classroom, she realized she had left her history book on her desk.

To her horror, when she walked back into the room to get her book, she saw the same spidery writing that had appeared in her notebook scrawled in huge letters on the chalkboard at the front of the room.

Maddie's legs were shaking. "Who's writing this? What do you want from me?" she cried as she looked around the room.

When her eyes returned to the chalkboard, she saw two new letters in the lower corner. The letters were **entwined**.

Maddie turned and ran outside the door. Just as she was heading down the hallway, she bumped into Christa and Evie.

"Hey Maddie, what's going on? We've been waiting for you outside," said Evie. "We're going for hot chocolate."

Maddie hid her face behind her long blond hair so Christa and Evie wouldn't see she was upset. She didn't want to share what was going on with anyone—not even her new friends. She wiped a tear from her cheek with the back of her hand.

"Hot chocolate sounds great," she said, forcing a smile.

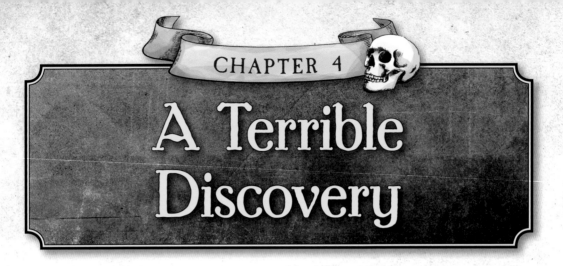

CHAPTER 4

A Terrible Discovery

"Breakfast is ready," shouted Mom.

Maddie was shivering. She squirmed in her bed and tried to pull the quilt over her shoulders, but it wouldn't budge. She sat up and saw that it was pinned under Max's huge, furry body. Her eyelids felt heavy as she thought back to last night. She had been up until midnight thinking about what had happened in Mr. Martin's class and called Max into her bedroom for company. Once she was snuggled up to the big warm dog, she'd eventually dozed off.

"Get moving, Maddie!" called Mom. "We have less than an hour to get to school."

School on a Saturday? Maddie's head was still fuzzy from sleep. Then she remembered—the tryouts for Lakeside's swim team were today. Suddenly, she felt energized. At her old school, she'd been one of the swim team's star **athletes**. Maddie couldn't wait to get back into the pool.

Maddie was standing at the edge of the pool. The water shimmered and her nostrils were filled with the scent of **chlorine**.

When the coach blew her whistle, Maddie and several other swimmers dove into the pool. Maddie's arms cut through the water. Within seconds, she was pulling ahead of the other swimmers. She heard her mom cheering from the **bleachers**. At the far end of the pool, she performed a perfect flip turn and began swimming back in the other direction.

That's when she heard the familiar voice.

"Maddie. Please come find me."

Maddie missed her stroke and swallowed a large gulp of water. It was the same whispering voice she had heard in the music room, but now it seemed to be inside her head.

She ignored the voice and kept on swimming. Then out of nowhere, she felt something touch her leg. It was freezing cold. Then five icy fingers slowly wrapped around her calf. She kicked hard and tried to keep moving through the water, but the fingers were tightening around her flesh.

"Maddie, Maddie," whispered the voice as the **frigid** hand tugged on her leg.

A terrible feeling of cold spread throughout Maddie's body.

She began to panic and her head sank beneath the water's surface. Her nose filled with water, and she couldn't breathe. Maddie's head was spinning as she began to sink down and down.

"Please Maddie," pleaded the voice. *"Please come find me."*

"Come find me at the lake."

Suddenly, Maddie was yanked up to the water's surface. Choking and gasping for air, she realized her coach had jumped into the pool and was towing her to safety.

"Maddie, Maddie. Are you okay?" yelled her mom, crouching at the edge of the pool.

Maddie breathed heavily as her coach helped her climb out of the pool. "I'm okay. I . . . I just messed up," she said, quietly. "I swallowed some water and panicked."

While Maddie was riding home with her mom, her mind was racing.

Mary Carter—the lost girl who played the piano . . . the voice in the music room . . . the initials MC on the chalkboard . . . the icy hand in the pool . . . the voice that said, "Come find me at the lake."

Suddenly, it all clicked. Maddie knew what she had to do.

That evening, Maddie went for a walk with her mom and Max around the lake. "I have something to tell you, Mom. I know it sounds crazy . . . but you have to listen," she said. Then Maddie told her mom about the music room, the mysterious footsteps, the notebook, and the voice. Maddie described every strange detail.

Finally, Maddie said, "I think the lost girl, Mary Carter, died here, Mom. I think she drowned in the lake."

Maddie hesitated. Then she said to her mom, "Can Max try to find her?"

Mom walked for a few minutes without saying a word. Then she turned to Maddie and said, "It's highly unlikely that we'll find anything, sweetie. The girl went missing a long time ago. But, if it would make you feel better, we can try."

Mom gave Max's head a rub. "Okay—time to work, Max," she said. The big dog was immediately **alert**. "Find Zeeky."

This was Max's command word, which Maddie's mom had made up. Once Max heard this special command, he knew he should search for a dead body.

Max trotted off along the edge of the lake. Without speaking, Maddie and her mom quickly followed. Max zigzagged back and forth as he moved along the shore of the lake.

Then, Max bolted out onto a small wooden pier that jutted into the lake. He looked over the edge of the pier and sniffed the air above the water. Then, he walked to the very end of the pier and lay down.

"Max," shouted Mom. "Come here, boy." But Max wouldn't leave his spot at the end of the pier.

Maddie looked at her mom. She didn't dare say a word.

"I don't believe it," said Mom. "He's found something. There's something down there."

It was very early on Sunday morning. Maddie was sitting on a wooden bench at the side of the lake. She sank her fingers into Max's thick fur. He looked up at her and wagged his tail. "You did great, Max," she whispered.

Maddie's mom **emerged** from the crowd of police officers gathered on the pier. As she walked toward Maddie, she gave her daughter a tired smile.

"Well, Maddie," she said. "I still can't believe it, but the police divers have found something."

Mom looked **solemn**. "They've found a body . . . a skeleton. It's very old and has been buried in the mud under the pier for many years."

Mom hesitated. "They think it's a young girl."

Maddie could hardly believe what she was hearing. But in her heart she'd known since last night what they would find.

"Is it Mary Carter?" she asked quietly.

"I think so," answered her mom. "We'll know for sure after some tests, but look at this."

Maddie's mom held out a plastic bag. It was the kind that police officers use for keeping **evidence** safe. "We found this near the skeleton."

Maddie looked at the bag. It contained a gold chain covered with slimy green **algae** from the lake. Attached to the chain were two delicate gold letters that

were entwined, just like the letters that had appeared on the chalkboard. Now that her body had been found, Maddie hoped that Mary Carter would finally find peace.

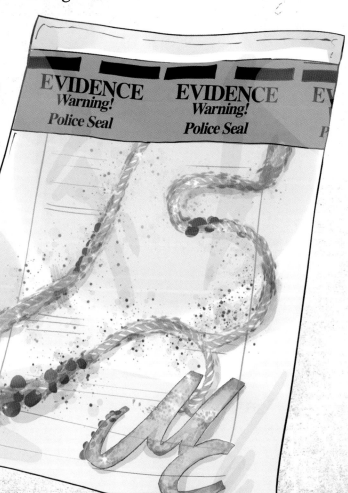

The Ghostly Secret of Lakeside School

1. In what ways is Lakeside Middle School different from Maddie's previous school?

2. What does Maddie find out about Mary Carter from the old newspaper story?

3. What do Maddie and Mary Carter have in common?

4. How does Mary Carter try to contact Maddie? Use examples from the story to explain.

5. Why do Maddie, her mom, and the police believe that the skeleton under the pier is Mary Carter? Use clues from the story to explain.

GLOSSARY

alert (uh-LURT) to pay attention

algae (AL-gee) tiny plantlike living things often found in lakes, ponds, and other bodies of water

athletes (ATH-leets) people who are trained in or are very good at sports

bleachers (BLEE-churz) raised seats or benches

briskly (BRISK-lee) quickly and actively

chlorine (KLOR-een) a chemical with a strong smell that is added to water to kill harmful germs

claustrophobic (*klawss*-truh-FOH-bik) afraid of being in small, enclosed places

dread (DRED) fear

emerged (i-MURJD) came out from somewhere hidden

entwined (en-TWAHYND) wound or twisted together

evidence (EV-uh-duhnss) facts or materials that give proof that a crime has taken place

flush (FLUHSH) to become red and warm

frantically (FRAN-tik-lee) to do something with worry or fear

frigid (FRIJ-id) extremely cold

implausible (im-PLAW-suh-buhl) not reasonable or probable

modern (MOD-urn) having to do with the present time

search-and-rescue (SURCH-AND-RES-kyoo) to look for missing people who are in distress or danger

ABOUT THE AUTHOR

Dee Phillips develops and writes nonfiction books for young readers and fiction books—including historical fiction—for middle graders and young adults. She loves to read and write stories that have a twist or an unexpected, thought-provoking ending. Dee lives near the ocean on the southwest coast of England. A keen hiker, her biggest ambition is to one day walk the entire coast of Great Britain.

ABOUT THE ILLUSTRATOR

Amit Tayal is a self-taught comic and children's book illustrator originally from Delhi, India. His creative adventure began at age seven when he used to trade his superhero sketches with friends in return for help with his homework. In more recent times, Amit has worked for publishing houses producing a variety of work from cute children's books to gritty, dark illustrations for games and comics. Amit loves to draw all types of illustrations. He is best known for his award-winning graphic novel titles: *Steve Jobs: Genius by Design*, *The Jungle Book*, and *Super Sikh*, the first modern Sikh comic book superhero.